Clover Kitty Goes to Kittygarten

By Laura Purdie Salas · Illustrated by Hiroe Nakata

two lions

Published by Two Lions, New York
www.apub.com

Amazon, the Amazon logo, and Two Lions are trademarks of Amazon.com, Inc., or its affiliates.

ISBN-13: 9781542042468 (hardcover)
ISBN-10: 1542042461 (hardcover)

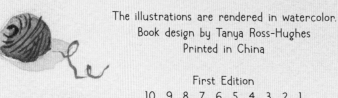

The illustrations are rendered in watercolor.
Book design by Tanya Ross-Hughes
Printed in China

First Edition
10 9 8 7 6 5 4 3 2 1

For Joyce Sidman, Mary Bevis, Michelle Myers Lackner,
Tracy Nelson Maurer, and Tunie Munson-Benson—
wordsmiths and friends through ups and downs
—L. P. S.

To Koharu
—H. N.

Clover Kitty liked calm things.
Knitting mittens. Nibbling kibble.
Catnapping on a warm floor.
Sometimes she wished she had a friend
to knit or nibble or nap with.
But mostly, life was purrrrrfect.

Until . . .

. . . one Monday morning, Mama Kitty announced,
"Do you remember what today is? The first day of kittygarten!
Are you ready for friends and games and songs?"

Pictures of high fives and curly slides,
dusty chalk and gluey paws
filled Clover's head.

She was **NOT** ready!

But quicker than a whisker twitch, Clover found herself
cowering in Ms. Snappytail's classroom.

Blocks clattered.
Neon numbers crowded the walls.
Sunshine glared through the window.

A paw touched Clover's shoulder, and she flinched.
"Hi, I'm Oliver," said the kitty.
Clover's mouth was dry as cotton.
She couldn't meow a single word.
Oliver smiled anyway.

Ms. Snappytail flashed spotlights off and on.

"Time for counting."

Next, she rang a bell.
But to Clover it sounded
like a **GONG!**

"Circle time!"

Then she forced the kitties to sit
on the crowded story time rug.

Kittygarten was a cat-astrophe!

At recess, Oliver came over and asked softly,
"Do you want to seesaw with me?"
Before she could answer, a squealing tornado
of fangs and fur circled Clover.

"You be a princess,
and I'll rescue you!"

Clover looked blank.
She shrank.
Clover's heart sank.

"Catch, Clover!"

At lunch,
the cafeteria lights
blinded Clover.

"Do you like juice, Clover?"
asked Oliver.

"Catnip cookies!"

"MILK!"

"Who wants to trade tuna
for my spaghetti?"

Clover grabbed.

She jabbed.

Her tiny claws stabbed.

Clover could not wait
for nap time.

But nap time was a disaster.
Ms. Snappytail's purrrrrfume stank like licorice.
"Sweet dreams, Clover," said Oliver.

"Nap time!" "Share my rug!" "Rock-a-bye, kitty, in the treetop . . ."

A treetop! Clover's belly swayed, and she couldn't sleep
on her scratchy mat. She tried. She sighed.
Clover Kitty quietly cried.

School felt nine lives long.
Maybe ten.

After nap time, Ms. Snappytail marched the kitties
through school like prisoners.

A tail touched Clover's face!
In her purrrrrsonal space!

THAT

WAS

IT.

Clover spit.

She bit.

She threw a fur-flying hissy fit.

"I QUIT!"

Clover fled.

"See you tomorrow, Clover?"
asked Oliver.

It took Clover furever to reach home.
"You look like you had an exciting day!" said Mama.
Then her whiskers drooped. "Are you okay, Clover?"

Without a meow, Clover curled into a circle.
Mama rubbed just behind Clover's left ear
until Clover fell asleep.

Tuesday morning, Clover said, "Mama, I feel sick
from icky catnip cookies."
"All right," Mama said. "No kittygarten today."
Clover snoozed all morning in her soothing room.

Later, Oliver Kitty stopped by.
"We miss Clover," he said to Mama.
"She's resting," said Mama. "You'll see her tomorrow."
Clover was playing checkers alone in her closet. (She won.)
"Whew!" she said when Oliver left.

Wednesday morning, Clover was still . . . sick.
"Are you sure?" Mama asked.
"I'm sure," Clover said.

Oliver came back that afternoon.
Mama said, "Clover is still resting.
But you may say hi."

Oliver searched Clover's room, but Clover was not there.
When Oliver gave up and left, Clover sighed in relief.
Although . . . a hollow twinge twanged in her chest.

Thursday morning, Clover was almost better.
"Ekh-ekh," she almost coughed. "I'm too sick for school,
but I feel just well enough to seesaw."
"Are you sure?" Mama asked.
"Pawsitive," Clover said.
"Okay, but tomorrow you will go to kittygarten."
"Ekh-ekh," Clover said.

Seesawing by herself had its ups and downs. (Mostly downs.)
Clover watched for Oliver. He didn't come.
What would it be like to play with a friend? Clover wondered.

But she did not miss kittygarten . . .
. . . did she?

On Friday morning, Clover was ready to try kittygarten again.
"I'm so glad!" Mama said.

Clover stuffed her backpack with survival gear.
She used sunglasses when Ms. Snappytail flashed the spotlights.
Earmuffs to soften the circle time gong.
And her own silky knitted rug for story time.

At recess, Clover played checkers with Oliver.
Then she needed alone time.

At lunch, Clover nibbled cheese and sipped juice.

At nap time, Clover slept next to her new friend, Oliver.

On her silky rug.
With plenty of space
between them.

Clover's day wasn't purrrrrfect.
But it was not a cat-astrophe.
And when she came home, Mama rubbed
the spot behind Clover's left ear
and listened to her tales of her day.

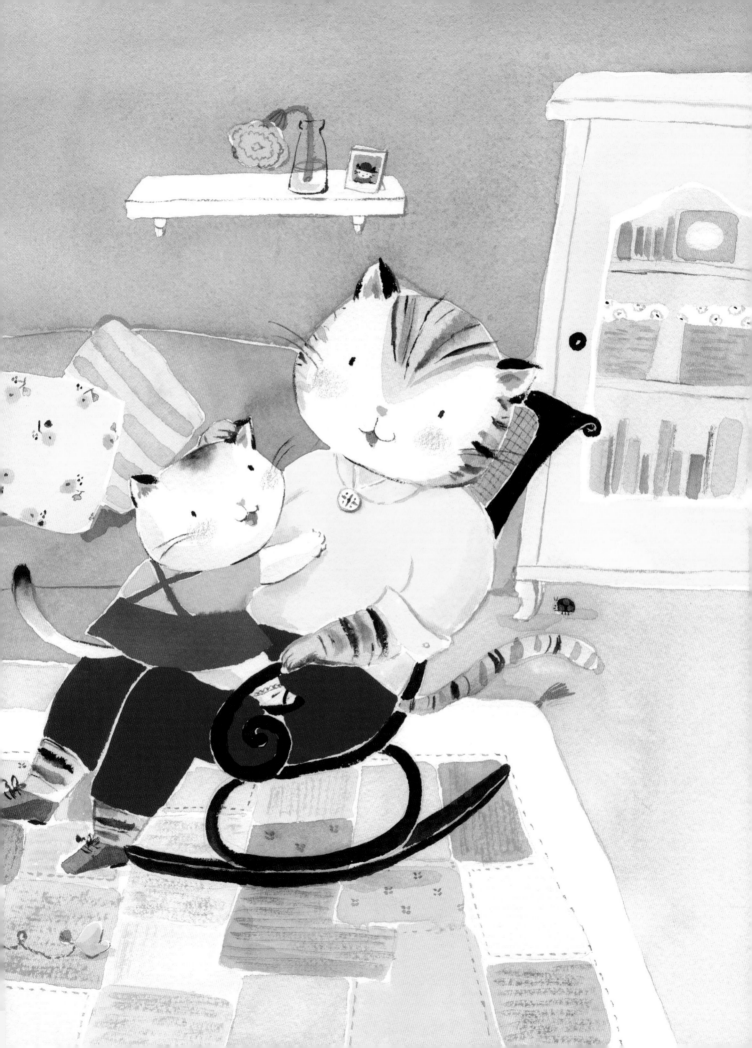

So Clover decided to go to kittygarten the next week . . .
and the week after that, too.
Each week got easier. It helped to have a calm,
kind friend like Oliver.

Meowadays, Clover can't wait to go to kittygarten.
And some days, she can't wait to go home.
Kittygarten has its ups and downs.
(Mostly ups.)